DEMI

THE
STONECUTTER

Crown Publishers, Inc. New York

Published by Crown Publishers, Inc.,
a Random House company,
201 East 50th Street,
New York, New York 10022.

CROWN is a trademark of Crown Publishers, Inc.

Manufactured in Singapore

Library of Congress Cataloging-in-Publication Data
Demi
The stonecutter / by Demi. — 1st ed.
          p.   cm.
Summary: A stonecutter wants to be everything he is not and has
to learn the hard way that what he really wants to be is exactly
who he is.
[1. Folklore—China.] I. Title.
PZ8.1.H6655St   1995
398.21—dc20
[E]   93-42413

ISBN 0-517-59864-7 (trade)
      0-517-59865-5 (lib. bdg.)

10 9 8 7 6 5 4 3 2 1

First Edition

A
LONG
TIME AGO
IN CHINA

there lived a stonecutter. One day a

rich man admired the stonecutter's skill

and asked him to work in his house.

When the stonecutter saw the rich man's house,

he envied him. He dreamed of being a rich man.

An angel heard the stonecutter's wish and turned him into a rich man.

Some days later, a governor passed the stonecutter's house in a big cart. The stonecutter, feeling very rich, put his nose in the air and completely ignored the governor.

Because of this slight, the governor ordered the
stonecutter beaten and fined 300 pieces of silver.

"Oh, dear!" sighed the stonecutter. "A governor is much more powerful than a rich man. How I wish I were a governor!"

The angel heard his wish and turned him into a governor.

The stonecutter was so proud of being such a powerful man that he paraded around in a big cart to show how important he was.

He happened to pass some beautiful white horses and wanted them for himself. He commanded his men to take them away!

The farmers were furious at this injustice
and came from all directions to teach him
a lesson. They caught the stonecutter and
gave him a good thrashing.

The stonecutter thought, "Oh, dear! Those farmers were worse than the governor. How I wish I were a farmer!"

The angel heard his wish and
turned him into a farmer.

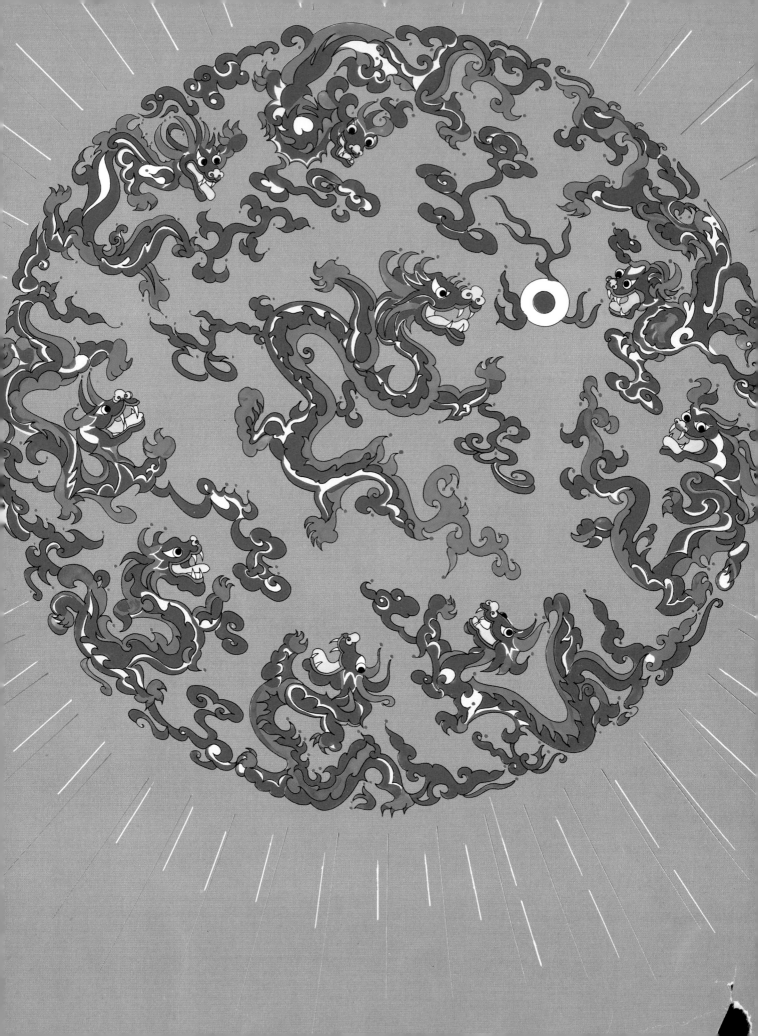

The stonecutter was happy for a while, but working under the scorching sun soon made him dizzy.

He thought, "The sun is much more powerful than anything on earth! How I wish I were the sun!"

The angel heard his wish and turned him into the sun.

But one day a cloud floated right in front of the sun and covered him up.

The stonecutter cried out, "Now I know that a cloud is much more powerful than the sun! How I wish I were a cloud!"

The angel heard his wish and turned him into a cloud.

But suddenly a gust of wind blew so fiercely
that the cloud was torn to pieces.

"Oh, dear!" cried the stonecutter. "I would
much rather be a gust of wind than a cloud!"

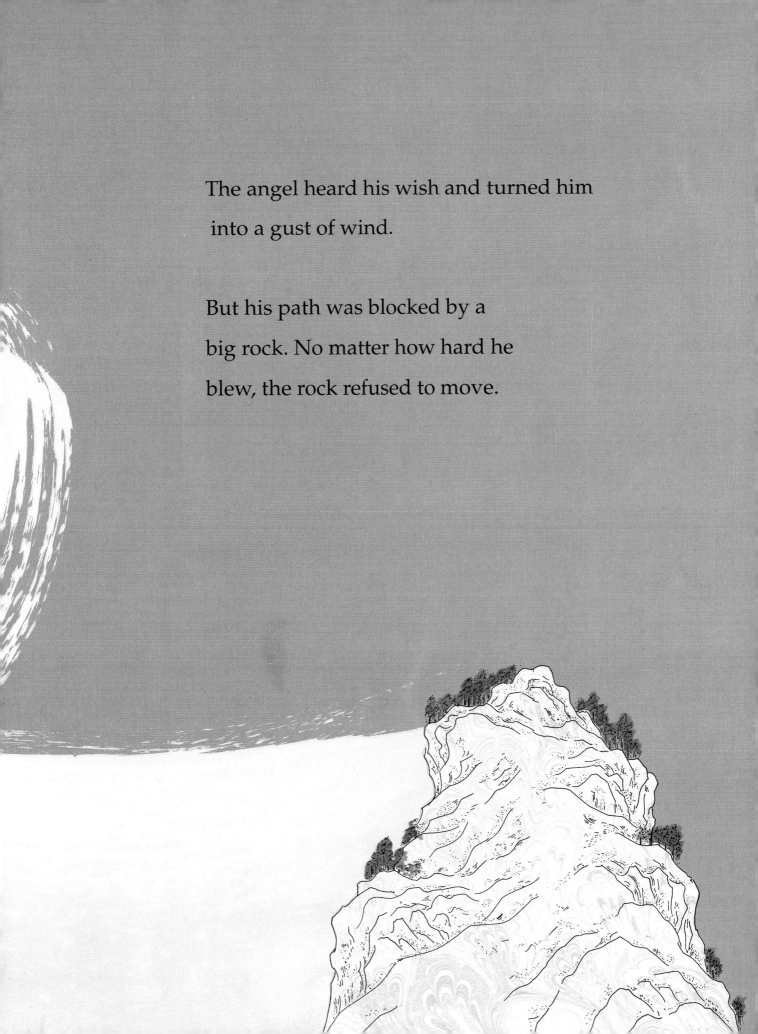

The angel heard his wish and turned him
into a gust of wind.

But his path was blocked by a
big rock. No matter how hard he
blew, the rock refused to move.

The stonecutter thought, "Oh, dear!

A rock is stronger than the wind. How

I wish I were a rock!"

The angel heard his wish and

turned him into a giant rock.

But after some time, stonecutters came and started to cut him up.

"Oh, dear! Oh, dear!" cried the stonecutter. "This pain is too much to bear!"

The angel heard his cries and, trying not to smile, said, "What do you want *this* time?"

The stonecutter was very ashamed of himself and said, "It seems to me that being a stonecutter is best after all!"

And so he was changed back into a stonecutter. He never wished to be anything else again, and carved the biggest and most beautiful stones in the world.

And he was very happy!